5-
MINUTE
MARY ENGELBREIT
FAIRY TALES

HARPER FESTIVAL
An Imprint of HarperCollinsPublishers

Mary Engelbreit's 5-Minute Fairy Tales
© 2018 by Mary Engelbreit Enterprises, Inc.
All rights reserved. Manufactured in China.
No part of this book may be used or reproduced in any manner
whatsoever without written permission except in the case of
brief quotations embodied in critical articles and reviews.
For information address HarperCollins Children's Books, a division
of HarperCollins Publishers, 195 Broadway, New York, NY 10007.
www.harpercollinschildrens.com

Library of Congress Control Number: 2017959286

ISBN 978-0-06-266326-9

Typography by Lori S. Malkin
18 19 20 21 22   SCP   10 9 8 7 6 5 4 3 2 1

First edition

CONTENTS

BEAUTY and the BEAST

NE DAY, A MAN SET OUT FROM home to seek his fortune. He promised his three daughters to bring back as many presents as he could and asked them what they would like.

"Diamonds!" said one.
"Dresses!" said another.

But the youngest, Beauty, asked only for a rose.

The man had not traveled very far when he came to a castle with a beautiful garden. It was filled with roses of red, pink, and yellow. Remembering his youngest daughter's wish, he stopped and picked a single flower.

As he did, a frightful beast rushed into the garden. "Thief!" the Beast roared. "How dare you steal my roses?"

"I'm sorry!" the man said. "I only wanted a rose for my daughter Beauty."

"You have a daughter?"
asked the Beast. He
thought for a moment.
"If your daughter willingly
comes to live in my castle,
I will spare your life.
But if she will not,
you will die."

The man was so frightened that he went straight home to his daughters. When Beauty heard what had happened, she said, "Father, we must not let the

Beast harm you. I will go." And though her father tried to stop her, Beauty went to the Beast's castle.

Beauty was frightened at first, but she was well cared for at the castle. She had only to wish for something—a meal, a dress, a jewel—and it appeared before her. In the evenings, the Beast came to have dinner with Beauty. He was frightful to look at, but she enjoyed his company and saw the gentleness of his spirit and the goodness in his heart.

Every night before leaving her, the Beast asked the same question, "Beauty, will you marry me?"

But Beauty always answered sadly, "No, Beast. I cannot marry you, for I do not love you."

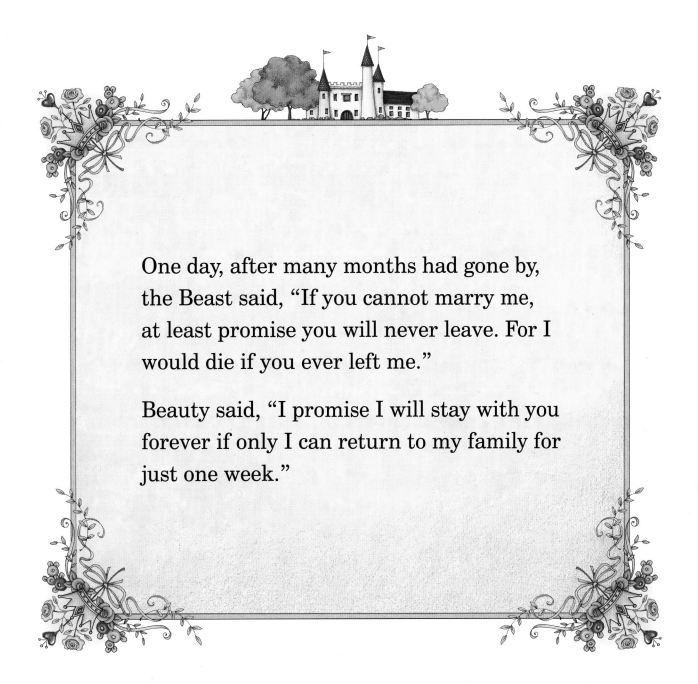

One day, after many months had gone by, the Beast said, "If you cannot marry me, at least promise you will never leave. For I would die if you ever left me."

Beauty said, "I promise I will stay with you forever if only I can return to my family for just one week."

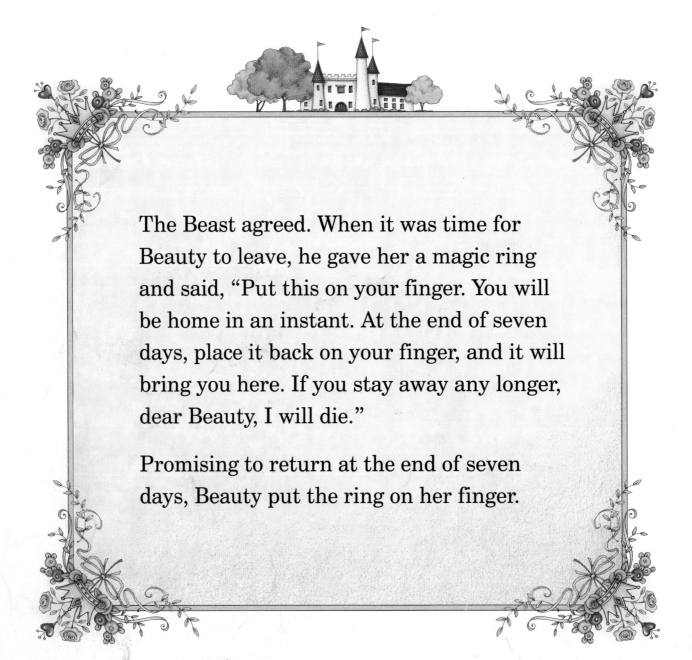

The Beast agreed. When it was time for
Beauty to leave, he gave her a magic ring
and said, "Put this on your finger. You will
be home in an instant. At the end of seven
days, place it back on your finger, and it will
bring you here. If you stay away any longer,
dear Beauty, I will die."

Promising to return at the end of seven
days, Beauty put the ring on her finger.

The next moment, she was surrounded by her family. So happy was she to be home that seven, then eight, then nine days passed before Beauty realized it.

On the tenth day, she had a terrible dream. In it, the Beast lay dying by a river. She woke, saying, "My poor Beast! What have I done?" And placing the ring on her finger, she was instantly back at the Beast's castle.

Beauty raced to the stream, where she found the Beast lying barely alive.

Kneeling down, she cradled his head. She whispered to him, "Oh, Beast. You cannot die, because I cannot live without you. I love you."

As she spoke the words, the light of the sun broke through the clouds and the Beast awoke. Then, right before Beauty's eyes, the Beast changed into a handsome young prince.

"A wicked fairy cast a spell on me," explained the prince. "I had to remain an ugly beast until I could find someone to love me for my goodness alone."

And then he asked the question he had asked so many times before: "Oh, Beauty, will you marry me?"

"I will," Beauty said. "I loved you even as you were, and I will love you forevermore."

And they lived happily ever after.

CINDERELLA

NCE THERE WAS A GIRL NAMED
Ella who was good and kind and beautiful.
Her father had died, leaving her in the
care of her stepmother, who was a vain and selfish
woman. Ella's two stepsisters were just as bad.
They made Ella do all the hard work in the house.
Every day, she had to scrub the pots, make the beds,
sweep all the floors, and clean the fireplace. Since
she was often covered in
dirt and cinders,
they called her
Cinderella.

One night, it was announced that the prince was having a grand ball. All the ladies of the land were invited. Cinderella longed to go, but her stepmother would not let her. Only her stepsisters would be allowed to attend the ball. That night, alone and lonely, Cinderella began to cry. Her tears were falling freely when her fairy godmother appeared. She asked Cinderella why she was crying. Cinderella said, "I want to go to the prince's ball. But my stepmother won't let me. I have nothing to wear and no way to get there."

Cinderella's fairy godmother smiled. Then, tapping a pumpkin with her magic wand, she turned it into a golden coach. She changed six mice into six fine horses, and a rat became a handsome coachman in a red coat.

Then the fairy godmother touched Cinderella with her wand. Instantly, instead of rags, Cinderella wore a pink gown and sparkling silver slippers. Cinderella was amazed. But the fairy godmother said, "Do not stay late at the ball, my dear, for at the stroke of midnight, the magic will end, and all will be as it was before."

When Cinderella arrived at the
ball, everyone stopped to stare.
Who was this beautiful stranger?
Her stepsisters, who did not
recognize her, were jealous. The
prince thought Cinderella was
the most beautiful woman he
had ever seen, and he asked her to
dance all through the night. As she
whirled around the ballroom, the
hours passed quickly. Too quickly.
Cinderella was having so much
fun, she forgot to think about
the time.

Bong! Bong! Bong! The clock began to strike midnight. Suddenly, Cinderella remembered her fairy godmother's warning. Leaving the prince, she ran out the door and down the palace steps. One of her silver slippers fell off, but she kept running.

As the clock struck twelve, her beautiful gown turned to rags and her coach disappeared! Instead of horses, there were now six tiny mice, and the handsome coachman was a rat once again. All Cinderella had left was one silver slipper.

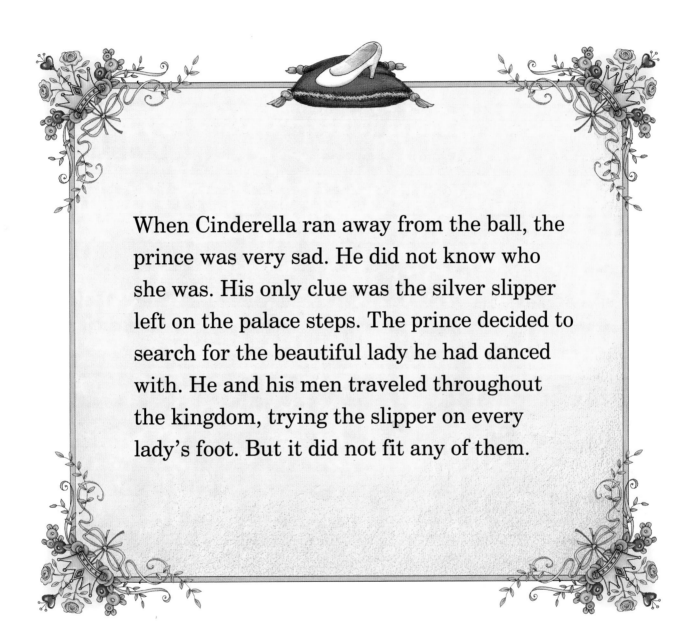

When Cinderella ran away from the ball, the prince was very sad. He did not know who she was. His only clue was the silver slipper left on the palace steps. The prince decided to search for the beautiful lady he had danced with. He and his men traveled throughout the kingdom, trying the slipper on every lady's foot. But it did not fit any of them.

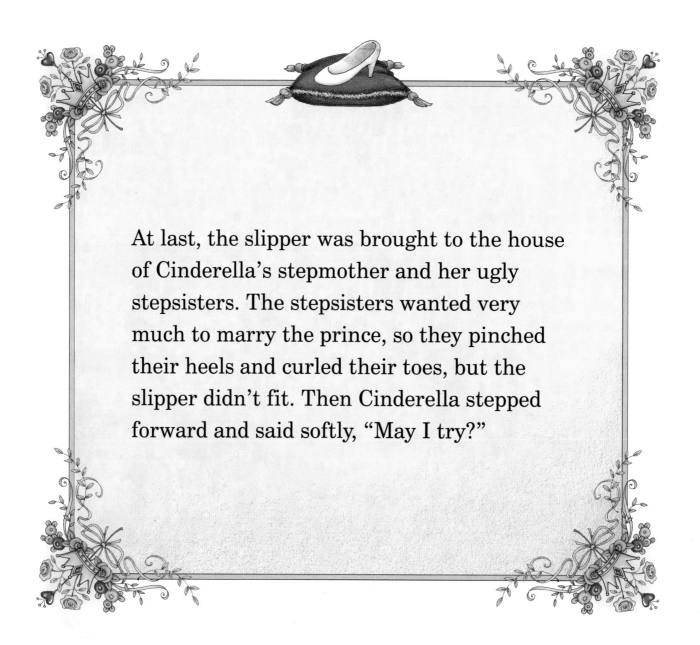

At last, the slipper was brought to the house of Cinderella's stepmother and her ugly stepsisters. The stepsisters wanted very much to marry the prince, so they pinched their heels and curled their toes, but the slipper didn't fit. Then Cinderella stepped forward and said softly, "May I try?"

The footman kneeled and slid the slipper onto Cinderella's foot. The prince ran in to find that the slipper fit her perfectly. Here was the lady he had danced with at the ball!

Then he took one look into Cinderella's good, kind face, and he knew she was his princess. It was a grand wedding. Cinderella and her prince danced well past midnight, and they enjoyed each other's company ever after.

ALADDIN

NCE THERE WAS A POOR YOUNG man named Aladdin, who was hopelessly in love with a sultan's daughter. Whenever Princess Aria passed by in her golden palanquin, his heart stopped. Aladdin knew that a poor boy could never win a sultan's daughter, but he swore that he would never love another.

Next to the princess, what Aladdin loved most was exploring. One day he discovered a hidden cave, and inside, he found an old oil lamp. It didn't look like much, but this was no ordinary lamp—it had been hidden in the cave by a wicked and powerful magician.

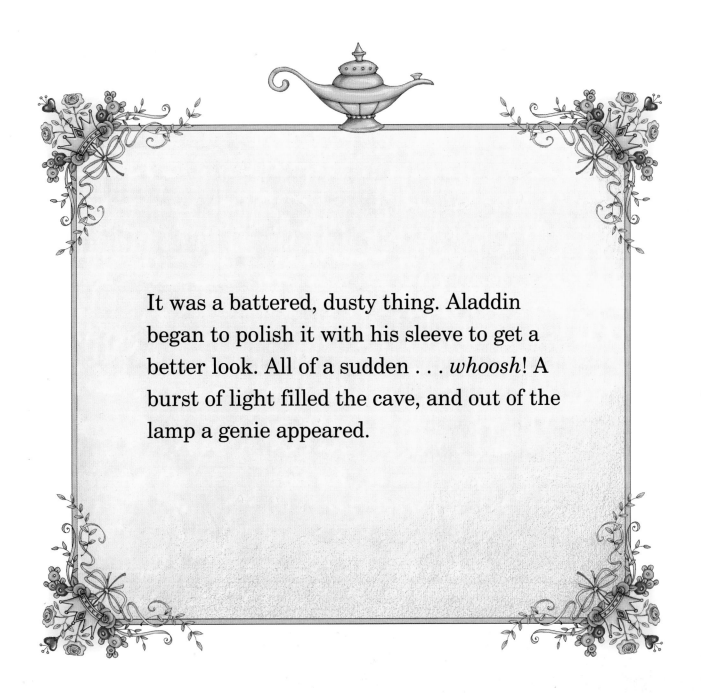

It was a battered, dusty thing. Aladdin began to polish it with his sleeve to get a better look. All of a sudden . . . *whoosh*! A burst of light filled the cave, and out of the lamp a genie appeared.

"Master of the lamp," the genie boomed. "What is your wish?"

Aladdin was astonished! And he knew just what to ask for. He said, "I wish for a gift fine enough for Princess Aria."

No sooner had he said the words than Aladdin found himself surrounded by riches. "Your wish is my command," said the genie. "What else do you desire?"

"I wish for fine clothes," said Aladdin, "and a good steed." His wish was the genie's command.

Soon, dressed in princely clothes and riding a fine stallion, Aladdin was off to the sultan's palace.

Aladdin was clever and managed to talk his way into the palace. Once he was inside, the sultan and his daughter were charmed by Aladdin's friendly smile. After an enchanting afternoon, Princess Aria agreed to marry him.

Aladdin commanded the genie to build a grand
palace for him and the princess to live in, and in
an instant, it was done. Happy beyond measure,
Aladdin still told no
one, not even his dear
Aria, about the magic
lamp he had found
in the cave.

One day when Aladdin was away, the princess
found the dusty lamp high on a shelf. Hours later, a
peddler came walking through the streets, crying,
"New lamps for old! New lamps for old!"

"Will you take even this old tarnished one?" the
princess asked.

"Certainly!" came the reply. For this man was not
a peddler; he was the wicked magician who had
hidden the lamp in the cave. And he was determined
to get it back.

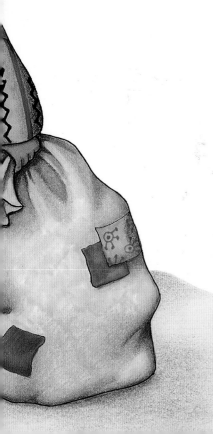

As soon as he
held the lamp,
he rubbed it,
and the genie
appeared. "Carry
this palace and all
of us in it far into the
desert," the magician
commanded. In an instant, only bare ground
remained where the palace had stood.

When Aladdin returned home, he realized
at once what must have happened.
Without wasting a minute, he set out to
find and rescue Princess Aria.

After wandering the desert for weeks and weeks, Aladdin discovered the palace. He snuck inside and surprised his bride. Aria was overcome with joy to see him.

"We must get the lamp," said Aladdin.

The princess said, "The magician keeps it with him always."

So that night, as the magician slept, Aladdin crept into his room. He took the lamp and made a wish. "Carry this palace and all but one in it back to the city." When the magician awoke, he was lying in the sand with nothing but empty desert as far as the eye could see.

Back in the city, Aladdin and the princess thanked the genie for all his help. The sultan was so happy that his daughter was back safe and sound, he gave Aladdin half his kingdom. From then on, Aladdin used the lamp only to do good for his people, and he shared his great riches with the poor.

SNOW WHITE and the SEVEN DWARFS

ONCE THERE WAS A LOVELY princess called Snow White. Her stepmother, the queen, was beautiful, but she was cruel and vain. The queen loved to look into her magic mirror and say:

Mirror, mirror on the wall,

Who is fairest of us all?

And the mirror always said:

Queen, you are fairest of us all.

But Snow White grew more beautiful as she grew older. One day, when the queen went to her magic mirror, the mirror said:

Queen, thou art the fairest that I see,

But Snow White is more fair than thee.

Furious, the queen called to her guard and ordered
him to kill Snow White.

The guard could not bear to hurt the innocent girl. Rather than kill her, he took her deep into the woods, where he left her. Returning to the castle, he told the queen that Snow White was dead.

Poor Snow White wandered lost and alone through the frightening woods for a long while.

At last, she came to a little cottage.

She knocked timidly at the door—and was surprised when it was opened by the tiniest person she had ever seen!

The cottage was owned by seven friendly dwarfs. When they learned what the wicked queen had done to Snow White, they offered to let her live with them.

Snow White happily agreed. Living with the seven dwarfs, she settled into a routine. Each morning, the dwarfs would go off to work, and each evening they would return to warm supper and a house as neat as a pin.

All the while, the queen believed Snow White was dead. Then one day, she stood in front of her magic mirror and said those familiar words:

Mirror, mirror on the wall,

Who is fairest of us all?

And the mirror answered,

Queen, thou art fairest that I see,

But Snow White living in the glen

With the seven little men

Is a thousand times more fair than thee.

Imagine how angry the queen was to learn that Snow White was not dead after all! Using her dark magic, the queen created a poisonous apple.

Then she disguised herself as an old
peddler and set off for the seven dwarfs'
cottage. Once there, she called out, "Apples
for sale. Delicious apples."

Snow White told the old woman she had no money.

"For one so pretty as you, the apple is free," the old woman said.

Snow White could not resist. She took the juicy, red apple and bit into it. As soon as she did, she fell down, still and cold.

The queen laughed with glee and disappeared into the woods. Now there could be no doubt as to who was the fairest of all!

When the seven dwarfs came home, they were heartbroken to find their dear Snow White lying on the ground.

She looked too beautiful to bury, so they placed her
in a glass coffin atop a high hill. Each dwarf took
a turn keeping watch over her.

Snow White lay there for a long, long time. But
her appearance never changed. She seemed only to
be sleeping.

One day, a king's son rode by and was charmed
by Snow White's beauty. He begged the dwarfs
to move the coffin so he could see her better.
As they picked it up, the bit of apple fell
out of her mouth and she awoke.

Seeing Snow White's lovely face made the prince
joyful. They walked and talked and soon fell in love.

The seven dwarfs were the guests of honor at the
grand celebration of Snow White's marriage to the
prince. A great feast was held, and Snow White
danced with everyone.

Before the night ended, she and the prince made the dwarfs promise to visit them often at the castle.

And so they all lived happily ever after.

RUMPELSTILTSKIN

NCE THERE WAS A MILLER WHO bragged about his lovely daughter to the king. The miller claimed that his daughter could do anything! "She can even spin straw into gold!" This was not true, of course. The miller didn't mean to lie; it just popped out.

The king was very excited. "Bring her to my castle," he said. "My advisers demand more gold."

So the miller brought his daughter to the castle. When the king saw her, he fell in love, but his advisers locked the poor girl in a room full of straw, saying, "Spin this straw into gold by morning. If you cannot, then your father will be put to death for lying to the king."

Now the poor girl knew she couldn't spin that straw into gold. When she began to cry, a tiny little man appeared. He promised to spin the straw into gold if she would give him something in return.

"My necklace?" the girl offered.

The little man agreed, and in no time, he had spun all the straw into gold.

The king was amazed and thanked the girl, but his advisers locked her into an even bigger room full of straw and demanded still more gold.

Once more the tiny man appeared. Again he promised to spin the gold in return for something.

"My ring?" the girl offered.

The little man agreed, and again he spun every bit of straw into gold.

The king was thrilled, but his advisers demanded still more gold. "Fine," he said, "but if she spins the gold again, I'll make that girl my queen."

Again the little man appeared, but now the girl had nothing left to give him.

"I will spin the gold," said the little man, "if you promise to give me your firstborn child."

The girl believed she would never have a child because she thought the advisers would keep her spinning forever and would never let her marry.

"Very well," she said. "I agree."

When the king's advisers saw all
the gold, they were at last satisfied.
And when the king embraced the
miller's daughter, he swore that
he would love her always. They
were married, and in time, the
new queen gave birth to a baby
boy, who was the joy of her
life. But on the boy's
first birthday, the tiny
little man appeared
once more.

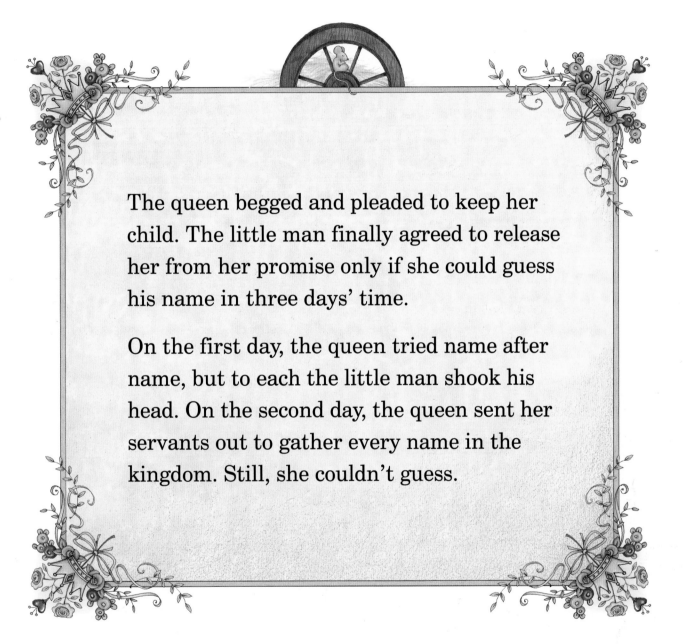

The queen begged and pleaded to keep her child. The little man finally agreed to release her from her promise only if she could guess his name in three days' time.

On the first day, the queen tried name after name, but to each the little man shook his head. On the second day, the queen sent her servants out to gather every name in the kingdom. Still, she couldn't guess.

On the third day, she had almost given up hope when one of her handmaids came running into the room. She had been walking in the woods when she overheard the little man singing:

What a most delightful game,

Oh, Rumpelstiltskin is my name!

That evening, the little man came to claim his prize.
The queen asked, "Is your name Peter?"

"No," he replied.

"John?"

"No."

"Ralph?"

"No!"

"Albert?"

"No!!"

Now the queen smiled.

"Is it Rumpelstiltskin?"

At that, Rumpelstiltskin stamped his little feet and flew into a rage.

He ran away as fast as his legs could carry him, and he was never seen again.

SLEEPING BEAUTY

N THE OCCASION OF THEIR FIRST baby's birth, a king and queen invited six good fairies to a grand celebration. But they forgot to invite the seventh fairy!

At the party, the fairies began to give gifts to the baby princess. The first wished her wisdom. The second, a kind heart. The third, great beauty.

And so it went up through the fifth fairy, with
each one offering a gift to assure the princess a
happy life.

Suddenly the door to the castle flew open. It was
the seventh fairy, and she was furious that she had
not been invited.

"Now I will give my gift to the princess," she said.
"When she is eighteen years old, she will prick her
finger on a spinning wheel and fall down dead."

Then the angry fairy stormed out of the room.

The king and queen were terribly upset that a curse had been laid upon their child. But then the sixth fairy, who was the youngest of all, stepped forward.

"I have not yet given my gift," she said. "I cannot change the wicked curse but I can soften it. The princess will not die but instead will fall into a deep sleep. And she will awaken only when her true love kisses her."

The king and queen were grateful to the young fairy
but still they worried. Trying to avoid the curse,
the king decreed that every spinning wheel in the
kingdom be burned in a great fire.

Many years passed, and just as the good fairies
wished, the princess grew to be kind and smart and
beautiful. The wicked curse was all but forgotten.

On the day she turned eighteen, the princess decided to explore the castle. Coming to a tower she'd never seen before, she climbed its winding staircase and opened the door at the top.

Inside was a woman sitting at a spinning wheel. The princess didn't know it, but the woman was the wicked fairy in disguise.

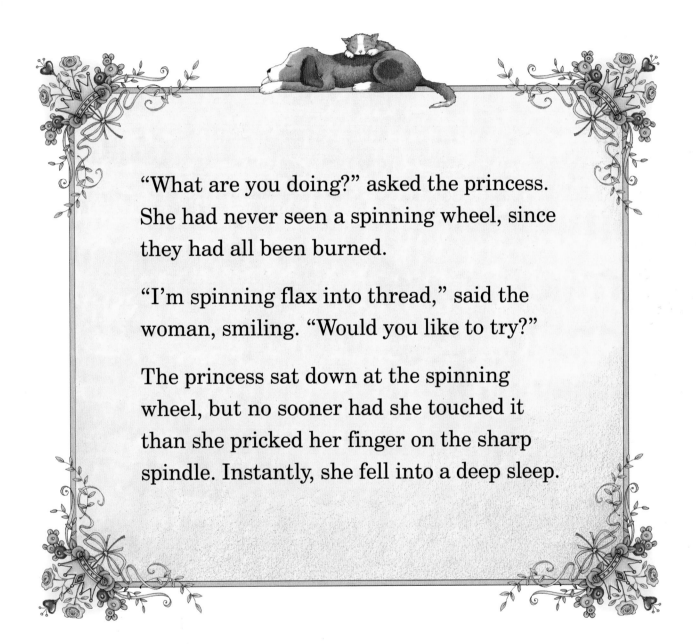

"What are you doing?" asked the princess. She had never seen a spinning wheel, since they had all been burned.

"I'm spinning flax into thread," said the woman, smiling. "Would you like to try?"

The princess sat down at the spinning wheel, but no sooner had she touched it than she pricked her finger on the sharp spindle. Instantly, she fell into a deep sleep.

In fact, the angry fairy's spell was so strong
that dogs stopped barking, flies stopped buzzing,
and curtains stopped flapping in the breeze. The
king and queen and every creature in the castle
fell asleep. A tangled hedge of thorns grew
around the castle walls, so thick that
no one could enter.

And then one day, a hundred years later, a prince came riding by. Over the years, many men had tried and failed to fight their way through the thorny hedge, but this prince was special. He was Beauty's true love. As he approached the hedge, its branches parted and he rode straight to the castle. Everywhere he looked, he saw people and animals fast asleep.

He tiptoed among them until, finally, he found the sleeping princess in the tower. He thought she was so beautiful that he leaned over and kissed her cheek. And just like that, the evil fairy's spell was broken.

Opening her eyes, the princess said, "I dreamed you would come." Then she took his hand, and they came down from the tower to find the whole kingdom waking up.

The king and queen were so overjoyed that they planned a great feast to at last celebrate the princess's eighteenth birthday. And this time, they made sure to invite every single fairy in the woods.

JACK and the BEANSTALK

ONCE THERE WAS A NOBLEWOMAN who had fallen on hard times. Her castle had been stolen away by a greedy giant, and now she lived in a cottage with her only son, Jack. He was a lazy boy—always dreaming, never working.

Mother and son grew poorer and poorer until they had nothing but a cow.

Jack's mother told him to sell the cow for a good price, and he agreed. But do you know what?

On the way into town, Jack met a strange little man, who gave him three magic beans in exchange for the cow.

Jack thought his mother would be happy to have the beans—after all, they were magic!

"Three beans!" Jack's mother shouted when he got home. "You foolish boy!" Disgusted, she threw the beans out the window.

Now Jack felt sad, and he went straight to bed. But in the morning, when he went to the window, he saw that the magic beans had sprung up into a huge vine! There was nothing to do but climb it.

Higher and higher he climbed, until at last he
reached the top of the vine and found himself
looking at a castle that was high among the clouds.

Jack didn't know it, but
this was the very castle
that had been stolen
from his mother when
he was just a baby.

When Jack got there, he knocked. A giant woman answered the door. After taking one look at him, she said, "Please, please run away! My husband is a cruel giant!" But Jack was exhausted and hungry, so he offered to work for food, and she let him in.

As he was finishing up his dinner, there came a deafening roar. Jack hid in the cupboard just as the giant thundered in, bellowing, "Fee—fi—fo—fum, I smell the blood of an Englishman!"

But the giant's wife said, "It's the stew you smell."

"Humph!" the giant grunted, and he sat down to his giant supper. At last he finished eating, and his wife brought out a golden goose.

"Lay!" shouted the giant. And the goose laid an egg of solid gold! The giant amused himself for hours, commanding the goose to lay her golden eggs.

Finally, the giant's wife brought out a
harp. The giant said, "Play me a drink!"
and a drink appeared. "Play me a pillow!"
and a pillow appeared in the giant's chair.
"Play music!" and the harp played lovely
music until, at last, the giant fell asleep.

When the giant was snoring loudly, Jack crept out of
his hiding place, grabbed the golden goose and the
harp, and started to run! But the harp twisted in
Jack's grasp and started chiming, "Master!
Master!"

Jack held tight to the goose and
the harp and ran to the beanstalk
as fast as he
could go.

But the harp's cries woke the giant. His feet shook the ground as he chased them! The beanstalk trembled with the terrible weight of him!

As soon as Jack was safely on the ground, he cut the beanstalk with one swing of his hatchet. The giant fell to the ground and died instantly!

Jack gave the golden goose to his mother, who instantly recognized it as her own beloved pet. Then he said to the harp, "Play dinner, please." A grand meal appeared before them. The very next day, Jack asked the harp to play a gown for his mother, a castle to live in, and happiness to last a lifetime.

PUSS IN BOOTS

NCE THERE WAS A YOUNG MAN who had nothing in the world but a cat named Puss. The young man felt very sorry for himself, and he sighed. "What good is a cat?"

Now Puss was a clever cat. And hearing this, he replied, "A cat is a very fine thing indeed."

"Give me a pair of boots and a sack and I will make your fortune," Puss said to the young man.

The young man agreed. As soon as Puss got his boots, he set off.

First he caught a fine rabbit and put it in the sack. Then he boldly made his way to the castle. "Let me in. I have come to see the king!" he cried. "I bring a gift from my master, the magnificent Marquis of Carabas!"

The king was so pleased with the gift of the rabbit, he invited Puss in Boots to stay for a grand supper. The cat ate his fill from the banquet table, and while he ate, he talked.

First he told the king how rich the Marquis of Carabas was.

Then he told the queen how noble the Marquis of Carabas was.

Then he told the princess that his master was handsome, brave, and charming.

By the time Puss in Boots left the castle, everyone was talking about the mysterious Marquis of Carabas.

While at the castle, Puss had learned that the royal family was about to take a tour of the countryside. He ran back to his master and said, "I have a plan. Go swimming in the river today, and I will make your wildest dreams come true."

While the young man swam, Puss hid his clothes. Then Puss jumped in front of the king's carriage and shouted, "Help! My master, the Marquis of Carabas, is drowning!"

Quick as a flash, the king's footmen jumped in the river and pulled the young man out. "Someone has stolen my clothes!" the young man cried.

So the king gave the young man new clothes to wear and let him sit in his own royal carriage. In his borrowed clothes, the Marquis of Carabas looked just as rich and noble and handsome as Puss had promised.

Next Puss in Boots ran ahead to the ogre's castle. He knocked boldly on the door and the ogre answered.

"Is it true that you can turn into anything you like?" Puss asked. "It is," said the ogre proudly, and to prove it, he turned into a lion.

"But it must be easy for an ogre to turn into a lion," said Puss in Boots. "There is no way an ogre could turn into something tiny, like a mouse."

The lion roared and turned into a mouse. In a flash, Puss ate him up, and that was the end of the ogre.

Along the road, the king saw the farmers working. When he asked who owned the land, the farmers did just as Puss had told them and said, "The Marquis of Carabas!"

Puss in Boots stood by the ogre's castle gate. When the king came by, Puss called, "The Marquis of Carabas welcomes you to his home."

The king and queen and the princess ate a marvelous supper in the castle with the marquis and his wily cat. Before long, the princess and the Marquis of Carabas were engaged to be married.

On the day of his wedding, the Marquis of Carabas turned to Puss in Boots and said, "Thank you, my friend. You were right—a cat is a very fine thing, indeed!"

HANSEL and GRETEL

NCE UPON A TIME THERE LIVED a brother and sister called Hansel and Gretel. Their father had died, and the family was very poor. Often, they only had stale bread to eat. One day their mother found that the cupboard was bare. So she sent the children out into the woods to pick wild strawberries for supper.

"The woods get dark very quickly," Mother said. "Be sure you don't get lost."

Now Hansel was a clever boy, and Gretel was a clever girl. As they walked farther and farther into the woods, they dropped a trail of bread crumbs to follow back to the cottage.

Working together, Hansel and Gretel filled their basket with ripe, red strawberries. By late afternoon, they were ready to go home.

"Mother will be so happy," said Hansel.

"But where are
the bread crumbs?"
Gretel cried.

The birds had
eaten every crumb.
Now there was
no trail to lead
the children
home.

Lost and afraid, poor Hansel and Gretel walked for a long while. At suppertime, they ate all the berries because they were so hungry. Trying to stay cheerful, the children made plans for the morning, then fell asleep on the forest floor.

When the sun woke them, Hansel and Gretel set off through the woods. They'd wandered all day long when they came to a clearing, and there they saw a wonderful thing. It was a little cottage made of cake and candy! Everywhere, they saw lollipops, gumdrops, frosted cookies, and chocolate. Hansel and Gretel knew it was not polite to nibble on people's houses, but they were so hungry that they started breaking off small bits of the house to eat.

Then they heard a strange voice whisper, "Nibble, nibble, like a mouse. Who is nibbling at my house?"

NIBBLE, NIBBLE, Like a Mouse, who is nibbling at my House?

Suddenly the door opened, and out
came a very ugly woman who was really
a witch. At first, Hansel and Gretel were
frightened, but the witch spoke so sweetly. She
invited them to supper, and the children were so
hungry that they went with her into the house.
Inside, the witch fed them a delicious dinner, with
all the foods and sweets they had ever dreamed of.

They were so full that they soon fell asleep. In the morning before they woke, the witch lit a fire in the oven. "The boy first," she cackled. "Then the girl." For it was true—the witch lured children to her cottage and then gobbled them up!

After the fire was lit, the witch grabbed the sleeping Hansel and locked him in a cage behind the house. After that she came back and put Gretel to work.

"Get up and set the table!" she screeched. "I'm going to have a feast!"

Now clever Gretel saw Hansel in the cage and realized that her brother was to be the feast. As she set the table, she tried to think what to do.

"See if the oven is hot!" the witch called to Gretel.

By now, Gretel had a plan. She walked over to the oven and said, "It is stone cold."

"That can't be," said the witch, poking her head into the oven.

Quickly Gretel gave her a shove and banged the door shut. Then she set her brother free.

Hansel and Gretel ran away into the forest. Before long, they heard their mother calling, searching for them. She was so happy to see her children that she wept with joy.

Then they all walked home together and sat down to eat. Never had their simple supper tasted so good!

The EMPEROR'S NEW CLOTHES

NCE THERE WAS AN EMPEROR who wanted the best of everything—the tallest castle, the biggest army, the funniest jester, the fastest horse, and especially, the finest clothes. Knowing this, a clever tailor decided to play a trick on him.

One day, the tailor came to the palace with his prettiest silks and satins. He showed everything he had to the emperor, but the emperor was not pleased. "Don't you have something better?" he asked. "Something nobody else has? I am the emperor, you know."

"In this bag," the tailor said slyly, "I have the finest cloth in the world. It is as thin as moonbeams and as light as air. Believe me when I say no one has ever seen cloth such as this."

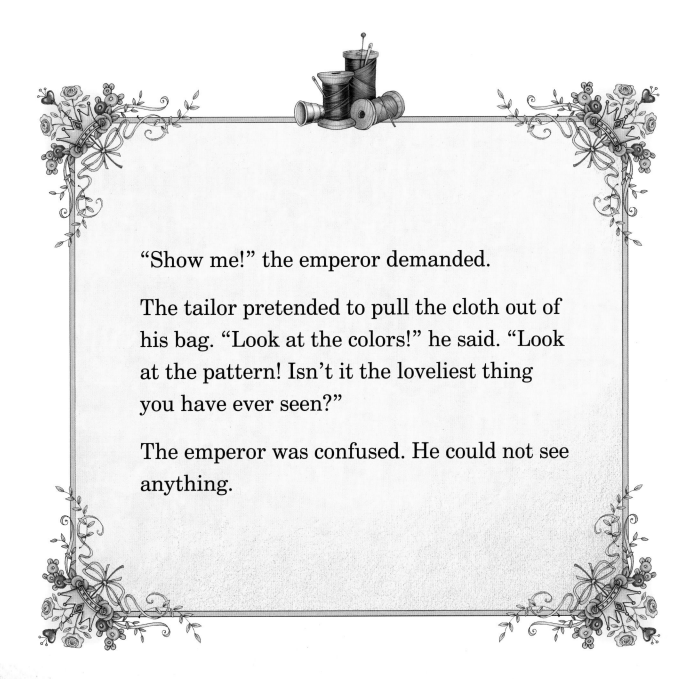

"Show me!" the emperor demanded.

The tailor pretended to pull the cloth out of his bag. "Look at the colors!" he said. "Look at the pattern! Isn't it the loveliest thing you have ever seen?"

The emperor was confused. He could not see anything.

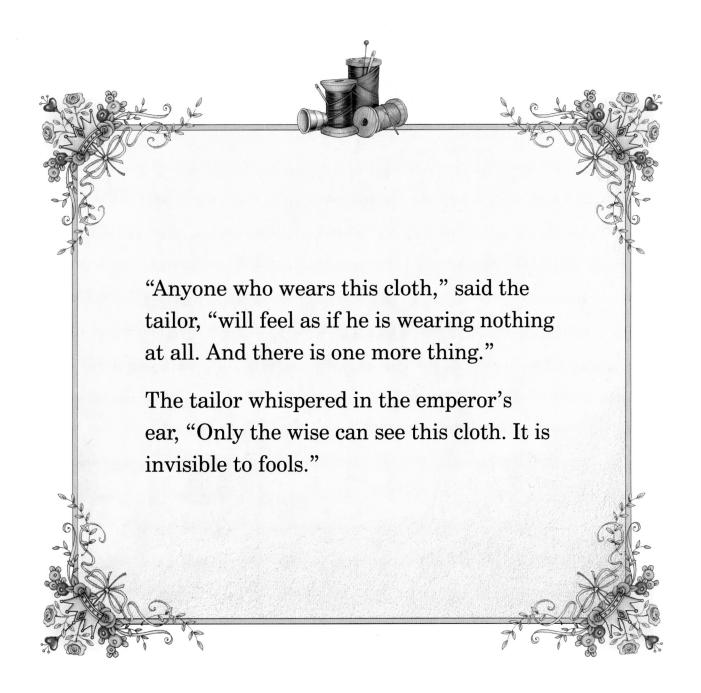

"Anyone who wears this cloth," said the tailor, "will feel as if he is wearing nothing at all. And there is one more thing."

The tailor whispered in the emperor's ear, "Only the wise can see this cloth. It is invisible to fools."

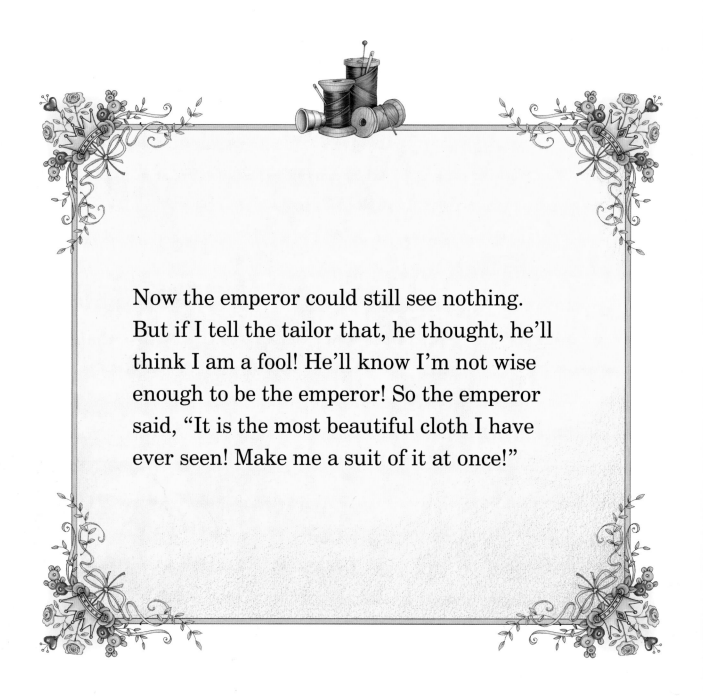

Now the emperor could still see nothing. But if I tell the tailor that, he thought, he'll think I am a fool! He'll know I'm not wise enough to be the emperor! So the emperor said, "It is the most beautiful cloth I have ever seen! Make me a suit of it at once!"

The next day, the tailor sent a box to the palace. Inside it, he said, was a suit made of the magical cloth. The emperor pretended to put the suit on and showed himself to the court. His wife could not see a thing. His servants could not see a thing. His soldiers could not see a thing. No one could see

anything but a man in his underwear. But they had all been told that only the wise could see the cloth, and fools could not. Naturally, everyone wanted the others to think they were wise. So they cried out, "Wonderful! Our emperor has the most beautiful clothes in the world!"

The emperor was so happy that he decided to go on a walk through the town to show everyone how wonderful he looked in his new suit. Now, the townspeople had also heard of the emperor's new clothes. They did not want to look like fools either, so they clapped and cheered as if they could see exactly what the emperor was wearing.

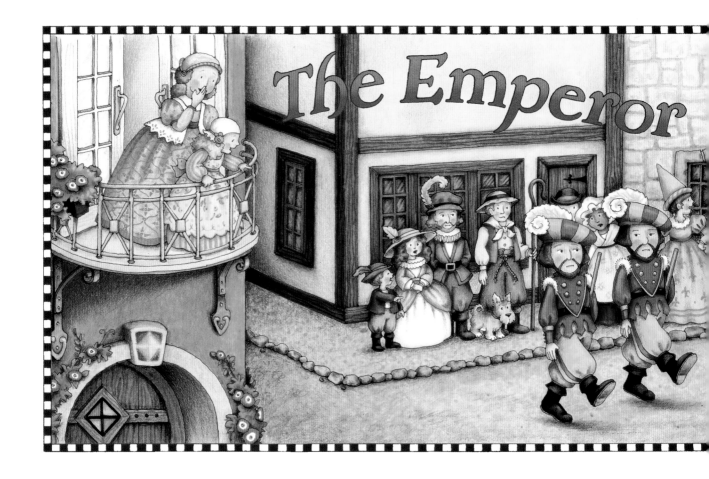

One little girl came onto her balcony. She could see
right away that the emperor had nothing on, and
that he was just walking down the street in his
underwear. She didn't care if people thought she was
foolish, so she said loudly, "But he doesn't have any
clothes on. The emperor has no clothes!"

The people in the crowd heard her. And they all realized that they couldn't see the clothes either—because there was nothing to see.

"The emperor has no clothes!" they shouted.

The emperor's soldiers heard. His servants heard. His wife heard.

"The emperor has no clothes!" They gasped. And the emperor heard. Then he knew how the tailor had tricked him. He rushed home to the palace. For many weeks afterward, he hardly dared to show his face. But after a while, he was able to see that he had been vain and silly, and that the truly wise can admit when they have made a mistake. And to this day, people tell the story of a foolish emperor who took a walk one day wearing no clothes at all!

RAPUNZEL

NCE UPON A TIME, THERE WAS an evil witch who stole a little baby from her parents. She named the girl Rapunzel and locked her in a tall tower deep in the woods where no one would find her. The tower had no door, no stairs, and only a small window at the top. Poor Rapunzel lived alone there for many years. Her golden hair grew so long it reached the ground.

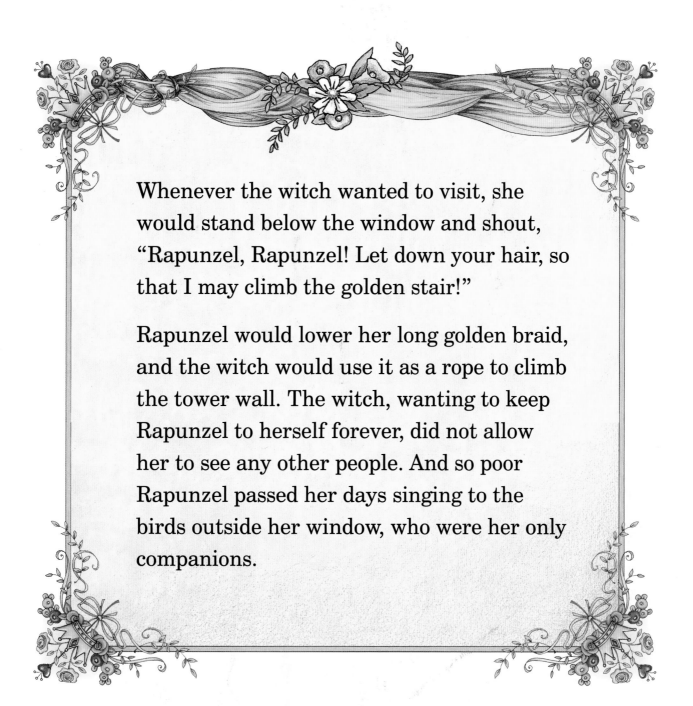

Whenever the witch wanted to visit, she would stand below the window and shout, "Rapunzel, Rapunzel! Let down your hair, so that I may climb the golden stair!"

Rapunzel would lower her long golden braid, and the witch would use it as a rope to climb the tower wall. The witch, wanting to keep Rapunzel to herself forever, did not allow her to see any other people. And so poor Rapunzel passed her days singing to the birds outside her window, who were her only companions.

One day, a king's son was riding nearby when Rapunzel was singing. Hearing Rapunzel's beautiful voice, he drew closer to the tower. At first, he saw no way to enter. But then he saw the witch arrive and heard her shout, "Rapunzel, Rapunzel! Let down your hair, so that I may climb the golden stair!"

Hiding behind a tree, the prince saw the golden braid cascade down from the window for the witch to climb.

That evening, as soon as the witch had gone, the prince hurried to the foot of the tower and repeated the witch's words: "Rapunzel, Rapunzel! Let down your hair, so that I may climb the golden stair!"

Thinking the witch had returned, Rapunzel did as she was asked. But she was surprised and delighted to see a young prince instead of the evil witch. She welcomed him happily, and they talked for hours.

The prince returned every evening to visit, and as they talked and sang together, they fell in love. They planned to marry as soon as Rapunzel could escape from the tower.

But one day, when Rapunzel was lost in dreams, she forgot herself and foolishly asked the witch, "Why do you climb so much slower than my prince?"

Realizing she'd been tricked, the witch grew furious.

Determined that no one should ever see Rapunzel again, she took out a big pair of scissors and lopped off Rapunzel's long braid with one mighty snip.

Then she took Rapunzel to a faraway wilderness and left her there, all alone.

That evening, the witch returned to the tower. When the prince called, "Rapunzel, Rapunzel! Let down your hair!" the braid came tumbling down as usual. But when the prince reached the window, instead of Rapunzel, he found the witch!

"Your sweet songbird has left the nest," she screeched. "You'll never see her again!" Then she pushed the prince out of the tower, and he fell far down to the ground below, landing in a patch of briars. The thorns scratched out his eyes, and he could no longer see.

Blind and lonely, the prince wandered far and wide, always searching for Rapunzel. He'd nearly given up hope when one day he heard a soft, sad song that he recognized from long ago.

Running toward the sound, he cried out, "Rapunzel!"
When she saw her lost prince, Rapunzel fell against
him, crying tears of happiness. And what happened
then was truly magical. When her tears fell into the
prince's eyes, he found he could see again! And what
he saw before him was his one true love.

Soon Rapunzel and her prince were married. Her golden hair once again grew long, and her joyous song filled their castle like sunshine.

THUMBELINA

NCE UPON A TIME, THERE WAS a tiny maiden named Thumbelina, who lived in a lovely garden where it was always summer. Only half the size of a thumb, she made her home under a flower. Her bed was a walnut shell, and she had a rose leaf for a blanket.

Thumbelina loved living in the garden. All of the bumblebees and dragonflies were her friends, and she often had them to tea.

One night, a toad was creeping through the garden. She saw Thumbelina sleeping under the rose leaf and thought, "What a pretty little wife she will make for my son!" Picking up the walnut bed with Thumbelina in it, the toad hopped away.

When Thumbelina awoke, she found herself on a lily pad far out in a stream. Two large toads were staring at her. The older toad told Thumbelina, "Meet my son. He will be your husband."

"Croak, croak!" her son said and tipped his hat. He was enchanted by Thumbelina.

But Thumbelina couldn't bear
to think of marrying the toad.
As the mother and son hopped
away, she began to cry. Luckily,
the fish who swam beneath the
water had been listening, and
they felt sorry for Thumbelina.
To rescue her, they sent her lily
pad floating far downstream.

Thumbelina sailed past many
towns, finally reaching a
beautiful country.

There she wove a bed from blades of grass, drank
dew from the leaves, and ate the honey from the
flowers. But when the winds grew cold and the first
snow came, Thumbelina had to take shelter with

a kind field mouse. "You poor creature," said the mouse. "You may stay with me all winter and tell me stories."

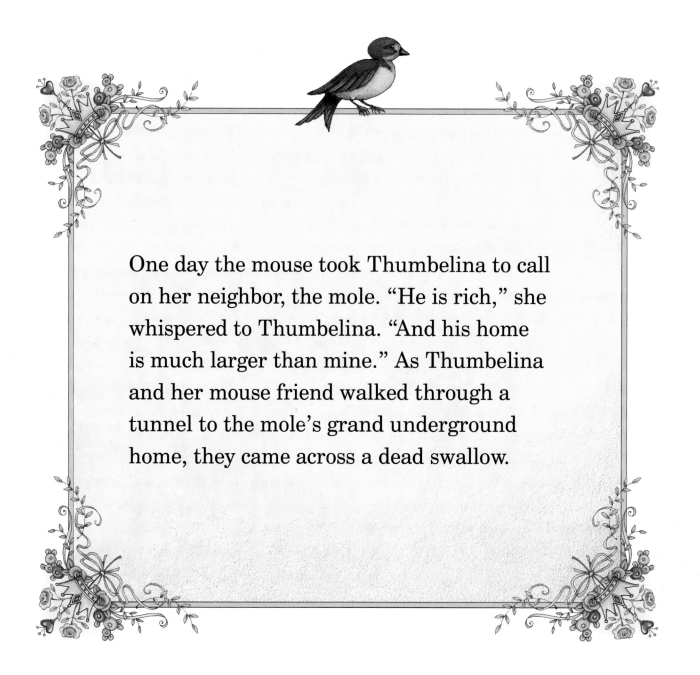

One day the mouse took Thumbelina to call on her neighbor, the mole. "He is rich," she whispered to Thumbelina. "And his home is much larger than mine." As Thumbelina and her mouse friend walked through a tunnel to the mole's grand underground home, they came across a dead swallow.

Thumbelina was very sad, but the mole just said, "He will sing no more now. How glad I am not to be a bird." He ordered his workers to cover up the hole in the tunnel roof through which the swallow had fallen. But he did nothing for the poor bird.

That night, Thumbelina could not sleep. Taking a
blanket, she crept out of bed and went back to the
tunnel where the bird lay. "Farewell, dear one," she
whispered. Spreading the warm blanket over the
swallow's cold body, she laid her head on the bird's
breast. But what do you think she heard then? The
thump of a heartbeat! The bird was not really
dead, only frozen—and the blanket had
warmed him back to life!

All that winter and
on into the spring,
Thumbelina secretly
visited the swallow,
bringing him food
and drink and
nursing him back to
health. Then one day,
she rushed to him
crying, "The mole
wants to marry me!"

Knowing Thumbelina didn't want to marry the mole any more than she had wanted to marry the toad, the swallow said, "I am well enough now to fly home. Why don't you fly away with me?"

Thumbelina quickly agreed. She climbed on the swallow's back, and away they flew!

Thumbelina and the swallow passed over forests and mountains. After many days, they came again to the land where it was always warm. The bird set Thumbelina down gently in a field of flowers. Here among the blossoms lived people just as tiny as Thumbelina, and they rushed up and welcomed her. Thumbelina felt warm and happy. After all her adventures, she had at last come home.